Movements of Magicalness

First published in New Zealand December 2020
by SHE Publishing, 30 Teddington Road, Governors Bay, RD1, Lyttelton. 8971, NZ

Contact: debs@movementsofmagicalness.com.

Cover design and book layout Barbi Larkins

Please visit www.movementsofmagicalness.com.

ISBN: 978-0-473-55875-8 (Pbk)
ISBN: 978-0-473-55876-5 (Epub)

Life is full of mystery and magic to be discovered. We each have a jewel inside that is ours to bring. We can discover what lights us up and fills us with joy and wonder as we reach for the stars.

Papatuanuku, our Earth Mother, showers us with her many gifts in all her forms—her many colours that enrich our lives and inspire us to create.

But when we forget to love, when we hurt inside, or feel lost and cannot find a clear way, we miss the treasures that are all around us. We miss our connection to each other, the animals, the birds and all the living creatures we share this life with. We forget to care.

In this book you will meet SHE and new friends who share their discovery of the magic through simple, still movements that unlock the deep mystery, as they open to the beauty and stillness within.

Deepest heartfelt love and gratitude for the Originator of CosmoForm, the profound moving meditation that this book is based on.

Who is SHE?

Some say she just appears, like a cat! No one knows when or how! Is it in the night or day? On a moonbeam? In the streaming of the sunlight? In the twinkle of a star? On the movement of a wave? In the song of a bird? The sparkle of a baby's eye? As the centre of the storm?

Who is she, where is she from?

What is her name you, ask. Luna, Flora, Oceana, Rosa, Maria? Or Skye with blue eyes? Pounamu, with eyes of jade green? Paua with her many colours? Aroha full of love?

Perhaps she has all of these names.

Or maybe, just maybe, she has none of these names at all! I say she has always been here. She is SHE!

SHE belongs everywhere and is of all things. She comes with Movements of Magicalness to remind us of our beauty, our stillness and our connection to all life.

Sam is sad.

Sam sits with his friend Jade. There is so much pain in his heart. Someone very close in his family has passed away. His mum cries all day and his dad gets angry. Sam feels so confused.

Jade has the Movements of Magicalness. They come through her heart and when she moves with them she knows a vast empty space full of stillness! She wants to share this with Sam, for him to discover this place and find that love in the Big Heart where all is good.

SHE knows the deep sadness that he is feeling. SHE knows that his tears belong to everyone that has ever been unhappy. We all feel it. We all share these human emotions.

Amber does not like the way she looks.

She does not like her red hair. Her pale skin burns when she is outside in the sun. She wants brown hair and darker skin, like her friends. They do not burn like she does and that makes her angry. She hates her friends for having fun, when she is quiet and sad! This makes her feel guilty and that makes her depressed and then she feels all alone. Nobody cares how she feels!

But she does know Movements of Magicalness and she is finding a new way. Closing her eyes, Amber breathes deeply and turns her palms up towards the sky. As she slowly moves them up, they meet above her head. This, for her, is her prayerful moment. This is when she knows the stillness.

With her eyes closed, she is discovering how peaceful it is and how her sadness starts to melt. With this magic she is discovering that she is as beautiful as any of her friends. She is perfect just as she is! If she can love herself, she can accept her friends for having fun.

Penina loves to stand in the shade of her trees under their branches and large green leaves. She meets them with her movements of magicalness. She feels in her belly and allows the warm glow to grow. Here in the Big Heart they are One, she and her trees, with all the insects and the birds and the hot shining sun.

The trees share their many secrets with her. She cares deeply for them and their big, colourful cacao pods. Inside each pod are rows of precious gifts for her to share. Penina and her family love their Koko Samoa and drink it every day. But she worries about the changing weather, the oceans that are rising and the storms that come, that they will damage her trees.

But the trees share with her, "Do not be afraid – we will find the balance. Here in the stillness, we know the way. We have the gift of cacao and you have the Movements of Magicalness!"

Aroha and Ben discover the power within.

Aroha and Ben look up at the stars in the night sky. The sky is vast and full of wonder and the stars sparkle and shine.

Keeping their fingertips together and opening up their hands, they make a little house above their heads. They call upon the power of the Universe for the great healing of their Earth Mother and all the Beings who share this home. They follow SHE as she whispers through the stars,

"This is the House of Great Goodness. What is it that you are discovering here?"

As she closes her eyes, Aroha is discovering that this house is full of mystery! In this house, the friends can feel the power of the moon and the sun and all the planets and stars. Ben knows that he is here because they are here, they are here because he is here.

They are discovering the true magic of life.

Manaaki dreams a cleaner world.

Manaaki loves surfing the waves and meeting the ocean animals. When he is on his surfboard with the wind in his hair and the ocean spray on his face, he is one with the waves and the movement of the water.

But it breaks his heart to see so much plastic floating by. It is a danger to his ocean friends and he knows it is not right to have their home full of so much trash. He wants to see and enjoy a clean ocean.

As he sits on his board, he moves the House of Great Goodness down in front of his body. He is knowing a depth and stillness within. He knows this as the ocean where all is possible. He sees that if we all truly care and value life, we can clean up our world.

Juan and Amarina give love to the forest.

Juan lives near the Amazon rainforest. Amarina lives in the bush in Australia. They love these places that are so alive with animals, birds, big trees and many beautiful plants and flowers. They know how precious all this is, but they see many bushfires. Juan and Amarina are very concerned about their forests and the fires that burn.

SHE feels their pain and shares her Movements of Magicalness. Slowly, together they tip their hands down to create a diamond shape in front of their hearts.

"Here is the doorway to stillness and healing for all beings" SHE whispers on the soft breeze. "Even in the fire there is new life." Their bodies tingle. Their bellies glow. They are knowing this truth within.

Here is the Big Heart where all can meet in love and know the gift of new life. Now they are full of hope for their homes, the great lungs of Pachamama, our beautiful Earth Mother, Papatuanuku.

Feeling sad is okay.

Sam moves with the magic that Jade has shown him. At first all he can feel is more pain, more sadness. He wants to stop these movements. It is too much, but Jade gently guides him through. She knows the magic. And SHE knows the power of facing our sadness.

Slowly Sam starts to feel something different inside. He feels the big embrace of SHE. He closes his eyes and hears HER words inside,

"Sam, it's okay to feel sad, it's okay for your family to feel the pain of loss. Be with it all, do not turn away. These feelings will pass. Stay in your heart; stay with the stillness. Find the love of the one who has passed in the Big Heart."

We are all One.

Zara had to leave her house and country. She has a new place to live in now that she wants to call home. But sometimes people are not very kind. They tell her she is strange and different and that her family do not belong here.

She so wants to be accepted for who she is, for the hijab that she wears. It should not matter what she looks like or where she is from. She wants her family to have friends, know love and be at home. With her Movements of Magicalness, she is knowing that, in the Big Heart, we are one with all our brothers and sisters – black, brown, white. We are One.

Haruko feels alone.

Haruko sits on the train from school and, although her brother and mother are with her, she feels empty and sad. They are not talking with her. She might as well not be here. Her brother is always on his laptop under his head phones and her mum likes to message people on her phone. City life is so full of busy people who do not see each other. They do not notice all the ugly towers that are popping up everywhere. She wants to find that happy smile she knows inside when she dances her Movements of Magicalness in the park. Here, in the park, she feels the water, the birds and the flowers. Here she feels connected to everything. It must be possible to feel this now with her family, she thinks. She would like to move with that magic now.

Jerome has so much to offer.

Where Jerome lives there are no trees. He would like to create a big garden with lots of plants and trees to nourish the sick people he knows. Or he could become a chef and learn to cook delicious food from his garden and teach people how to be more healthy. He could become a famous artist and sell his paintings of the things he sees around him. Or he could be a builder and help to build good houses for his neighbours to live in. He has so many dreams. In his Movements of Magicalness there is the House of Great Goodness where he feels so big, knowing the power of all things. He knows to bring this to his heart with the diamond shape and feel it deep inside. Now he has to bring his love to the Earth where he can make wonderful things happen for all to enjoy. "Jerome, you know all this is possible! You are here to create great things!" SHE calls to him as he brings his hands down to the Earth..

And to all, SHE spoke,
"Dear Ones, YOU have the Magic
YOU ARE the Magic.
Share this Magic for great healing. Shine your light. We are finding a New Way as the One Life, the One Love here on Earth. Be kind, be loving, be compassionate. Enjoy this life, create with your heart, inspire each other.

Movements of Magicalness

Join your friends here and become part of this movement of creating magic all around the world! They will show you the way, step by step as you move in your own meditation.

Remember: very slow, still movements, deep breaths and feeling in your heart is the best way!

Start by standing like Jerome, with your **hands by your side. Close your eyes.** Become aware of the air filling your lungs as you take **slow deep breaths**. This helps you to slow down your thinking and find your steady heartbeat. Feel the glow in your belly and the tingling in your hands and feet.

Turn your palms to face upwards as you raise your arms on both sides of your body very slowly. Join Amber with prayerful hands up above your head. This is where all things that seem to be separate come together. Pause. Take slow steady breaths. **Feel the stillness. Know that you are not alone.**

Next join Sam and Aroha in the House of Great Goodness by keeping your fingertips together and pushing out your palms to create the house. Pause. **Take a deep breath** and feel the house filling up with the power of the Universe. **Feel yourself expanding,** getting bigger inside. **Breathe deeply,** Feel the power the Great Mystery!

Join Manaaki as you slowly move the House down in front of you. **Discover the stillness** in this slow movement!

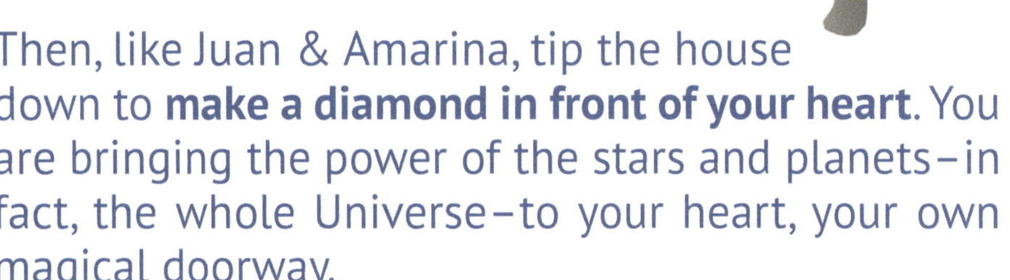

Then, like Juan & Amarina, tip the house down to **make a diamond in front of your heart**. You are bringing the power of the stars and planets–in fact, the whole Universe–to your heart, your own magical doorway.

Then, finally, join Jerome once more as you **bring your Love and Power through your heart doorway to the Earth.** This is your own special magic that you are bringing to your life and to all the living beings that share this glorious home with you.

Hi! I'm Debs.

I have been blessed to share these magical moments of meditation and contemplation with school children in the townships of South Africa where this book was conceived. With people around the world in drug rehab, in a New Zealand prison, after the Christchurch earthquakes and with our own children. Through these movements, wonderful connection is discovered, with a deeper love and care and knowing that we ARE the richness of this life - we are ONE.

It is my greatest wish to see a free life for all beings on this Earth. In co-creation with Barbi, we have given life to this book, a wonderful gift for you to share. I love this life, I know the magic that is here and I have so much gratitude for these simple but deeply powerful 'Movements of Magicalness'.

My name is Barbi. I believe in magic.

Magic surrounds us everyday, if we choose to take the time to look. As an artist and illustrator, I illustrate life both as I see it and as I imagine it. Life is eclectic. I like it that way.

Debs contacted me after seeing some of my more whimsical paintings in an exhibition in Christchurch. After an initial discussion, we knew we were onto something. From an illustration standpoint, it was an amazing collaboration. We started with some text and a single sketch. After that, the book took on a life of its own.

But then, life is what it's all about.

Visit us at
www.movementsofmagicalness.com